Oskar & Friends
In

The
Ravenhall Manor
Mystery

A Puzzle & Activity Book Experience
For Young Spy Agents

By

L.A. Edge

DEDICATION

To Oskar

CONTENTS

HOW TO PLAY

Take on this mission if you dare,
All you need is a curious flair.
Join forces with Oskar, if you're willing,
To unravel the mysteries of Ravenhall thrilling.

Puzzles abound, to enhance the tale,
But you need not solve them to reach the end trail.
Hints await at the back of the book,
So fear not, give it a good look.

Young and old puzzlers, this book is for you,
And yes, you can write in it too!
So pick up your pen, let the adventure begin,
And who knows what secrets you'll uncover within.

If you need the answers, go to:
http://www.PuzzlesAndActivities.co.uk/solutions

Good luck - and have fun!

CHAPTER 1. WHY ARE YOU HERE?

As you stand in the hall of Ravenhall Manor, waiting to embark on your adventure, you couldn't help but feel a sense of excitement mixed with apprehension. The grand manor loomed over you, its intricate details and imposing facade giving it an air of mystery and intrigue.

You had always been fascinated with spy stories, but never in your wildest dreams did you imagine attending a secret spy school. Yet, here you were, with your trusted friend Oskar by your side, ready to take on whatever challenges lay ahead.

Your parents had dropped you off at the manor, and as you looked out at the bay overlooking the sea, you couldn't help but wonder what secrets lay hidden within the walls of Ravenhall.

The invitation that led you here had come as a complete surprise. How did they know you were interested in spy activities and code-breaking? The invitation felt real, not like a simple game or pretend play.

As you stood there, thinking about the mysteries of the invitation, you turned to Oskar for answers. He looked at you sheepishly before pulling out a letter from his pocket. "I received this after the invitation," he said, handing it over to you.

You eagerly read the letter, which... made no sense at all. What does it actually say?

Puzzle 1. Who invited you to the spy school?

RAED RAKSO DNA DNEIRF

SA UOY WONK, I KROW ROF
A POT TERCES
YCNEGA NI EHT
HSITIRB TNEMNREVOG.

EW ERA GNIKOOL ROF
WEN SREBMEM
OT NIOJ SU DNA
I KNIHT UOY DLUOW
EKAM TAERG SEIPS.

LLA EHT TSEB,

ELCNU NIVAG

Wow, what an explanation! However, the letter raises more questions...

Puzzle 2. Where does Uncle Gavin work?

Perhaps by understanding where Uncle Gavin works, it will make more sense. Three words in the word search puzzle tells you where Uncle Gavin works. Can you find them? They can be found left to right or top to bottom.

K	H	F	R	I	A	W	B	I	K	X	P	R	A
G	C	T	Q	N	N	G	D	U	L	O	X	R	U
J	J	I	N	T	M	V	R	T	R	E	M	M	U
D	S	Y	D	E	A	W	Y	L	U	V	Q	H	T
B	T	D	B	L	K	C	K	Z	P	J	H	X	A
S	N	T	S	L	Y	R	G	C	A	E	O	E	B
U	O	I	D	I	I	C	S	E	R	V	I	C	E
F	Q	H	M	G	S	Q	F	H	B	K	L	D	C
N	J	S	A	E	Q	I	U	I	V	W	E	Z	R
P	E	R	B	N	H	W	K	Y	O	G	B	M	V
Z	B	O	F	C	V	D	S	E	C	R	E	T	K
C	F	O	T	E	W	B	R	U	J	N	R	E	Y

Uncle Gavin works at the

_ _ _ _ _ _   _ _ _ _ _ _ _ _ _ _ _ _   _ _ _ _ _ _

You couldn't believe it - you were part of a real spy mission!

Excitement and a hint of fear filled you both as you realised the seriousness of the situation. This was not just some pretend spy game, but a real chance to learn the skills and techniques of true espionage.

Oskar's eyes grew wide as he said, "My uncle must have seen something in us, something that made him think we were capable of being spies."

You nodded in agreement, feeling a sense of pride and determination building inside you. This was your chance to prove yourself, to show that you had what it takes to become a true spy.

As you looked around at the grand and mysterious Ravenhall Manor, you knew that the adventure had only just begun. The challenges, puzzles, and danger that awaited you would test your skills and courage in ways you never imagined. But you were ready for it - you were ready to become a spy.

CHAPTER 2. INTRODUCING FOUR NEW FRIENDS

As the sun started to rise, a lot of noise from the courtyard drew our attention. We hurried over to the window and saw a large bus pulling in.

Suitcases and bags were unloaded as four children stepped off the bus. They looked just as confused and curious as we were when we first arrived.

Who they were and what skills would they bring to the table? After all, they were chosen just like us.

"Shall we use our spy skills and observe them from here?" you asked Oskar.

He nodded and we began to take notes, carefully observing each of them as they made their way into the manor. It was going to be an interesting summer, that was for sure.

As soon as you lay eyes on Penny, you can tell she was no ordinary kid. Her wild, curly hair is like a bird's nest that's been hit by a hurricane, and her eyes are so bright and curious that you feel like you might be able to read a book by their glow alone.

She's the kind of girl who has a permanent twinkle in her eye and a mischievous grin on her face. Seeing her, you can't help but feel a little excited by the sheer creativity and energy that seems to come from her every pore.

Penny stood in the hallway with a lopsided grin on her face, looking like she had just stepped out of a science fiction movie. Her bright red suitcase, covered in stickers of robots and gadgets, looked like it was about to burst at the seams.

As Penny approached, dragging her suitcase behind her, she looked up and said, "I hope they have a workshop around here. I've got some inventions that need inventing!"

Puzzle 3. Penny

Let's find out more about Penny. Unscramble the words below which describe her and her interests.

IUCROUS ☐☐☐☐☐☐☐

EVCRAITE ☐☐☐☐☐☐☐☐

GEDGATS ☐☐☐☐☐☐☐

TROENVIN ☐☐☐☐☐☐☐☐

WHKSPORO ☐☐☐☐☐☐☐☐

Enter the words in the sentences below.

Penny has always been a _ _ _ _ _ _ _ and _ _ _ _ _ _ _ _ girl,

with a love for building and designing _ _ _ _ _ _ _ since she

was young. Her dad was an _ _ _ _ _ _ _ _ so perhaps this is

why she likes to make new things in her _ _ _ _ _ _ _ _ .

Penny is not afraid to fail and sees each setback as a chance

to learn and improve. Her skills will come in handy for spy

activities!

There is another girl who towered over most of the other children. She had a lanky frame, and the first thing that caught my eye were her big, black boots. They looked sturdy enough to hike through the toughest terrain.

As you look up, you see her practical outfit, a combination of different shades of green, which reminded me of the trees and leaves of the woods. It was as if she was preparing to blend in with the surroundings and become one with the natural world. Could you imagine her hiding behind a tree trunk, her long legs sticking out like branches? What a funny thought.

As Penny and Eva stood in the hallway, their eyes were drawn to a magnificent, towering fern. Its lush, emerald fronds cascaded down from the top of its slender, twisting trunk. Eva caught sight of a curious looking insect and couldn't resist inspecting it closely.

As she crouched down to get a better look, she noticed someone watching her with a puzzled expression. With a wry smile, she straightened up and turned to face the onlooker. "Sorry about that," she said, "I'm just a bit of a nature enthusiast. Name's Eva, by the way." She extended a hand in greeting, her face lighting up with a friendly grin.

Puzzle 4. Eva

Finish the crossword to find more about Eva.

Across

[2] A tall plant with a trunk and branches that grows leaves and often fruit

[4] A large area with many trees and other plants

[6] The skills and knowledge necessary to survive in the wilderness

[7] A tool with a sharp edge, used for cutting

Down

[1] A structure made to protect from the weather or wildlife in the wilderness

[3] An organization that teaches young people outdoor skills and leadership

[5] The ability to stay alive and healthy in challenging conditions

The words in the crosswords describe her and her interests - enter the words in the section below.

Eva is a tenacious and adventurous young girl who has a

deep passion for _ _ _ _ _ _ _ _ _. She loves nothing more

than being out in the _ _ _ _ _ surrounded by the natural

world, learning about the different types of

_ _ _ _ _ and the wildlife that calls them home.

With her trusty _ _ _ _ _ by her side, Eva has honed her skills in

bush craft and _ _ _ _ _ _ _ _ skills to perfection. She can build

a _ _ _ _ _ _ _ in no time. Her knowledge of bush craft which

she has learned through the

_ _ _ _ _ _.

Puzzle 5. Find the ladybugs

Eva had been busy admiring nature. Let's see what she found. Can you spot all the ladybugs?

Eva had introduced herself to the boy who stood quietly by the wall. He was lean and wiry, with a pair of glasses perched on his nose that gave him an air of quiet intelligence. His sharp and inquisitive eyes seemed to be taking everything in, as if he was always observing and analysing his surroundings. However, you could tell, Ethan was not shy, just seemingly observing us, with sharp and inquisitive eyes. With neat haircut and unassuming clothes, he wouldn't stand out in a crowd.

"I'm Ethan," he finally responded to Eva, his voice low and measured. "I like puzzles and codes, things that make you think. It's like cracking a secret code, you know? Figuring out what's hidden underneath." He gave a small chuckle then, and I could tell he was a bit of a jokester too. "And sometimes, it's just fun to see how far you can push your brain before it breaks."

As he spoke, every word seemed to be said with a deep sense of purpose, as if he truly believed that every code, every puzzle was a matter of utmost importance. It was clear why he had been chosen to attend the secret spy school - his intelligence and curiosity were palpable. Ethan's passion was infectious, and you know that he would be an asset to our group.

Puzzle 6. Ethan

What else could we glean from him? Fill in the missing letters to make up the words. Enter the words into the paragraph below.

M	R		C	D		A system of dots and dashes used to transmit messages over long distances
		C	R		T	Something that is kept hidden from others
	U	Z	Z			A game or problem that challenges the intellect and requires problem-solving skills
D	C	D	R			A device used to convert a coded message into understandable text
C	D	C	R	C	R	Someone who is skilled at deciphering codes and breaking secret messages

Ethan has a keen eye for detail and good memory and in his

spare time likes solving _ _ _ _ _ _ _ and making up

_ _ _ _ _ _ messages. He has not had the chance to be a

_ _ _ _ _ _ _ _ _ _, at least not yet. He learnt

_ _ _ _ _ _ _ _ _ _ _ from his mum who used to be in the Royal

Navy and has even built his own _ _ _ _ _ _ _ . He's very much

looking forward to making new friends and learning new skills

at the spy school.

Jose stood with his chest puffed out, exuding an air of confidence that was impossible to ignore. He wore a mishmash of bright colours that clashed in the most delightful way, and his clothes were adorned with what seemed to be every gadget under the sun. Wires poked out from his pockets like rebellious snakes, and a pair of headphones dangled around his neck, pulsing with an electronic beat.

When he spoke, his voice boomed like thunder and echoed off the walls. "Hey guys!" he exclaimed, his grin growing even wider. "I'm Jose". He pulled out a small device from his pocket and pressed a button, causing it to emit a series of beeps and lights. "Check it out! I built this baby myself. It's a portable hacking device. Pretty cool, right?"

Curious, you approach Jose to have a look at the device.

Puzzle 6. Jose

In the word search below, find 6 words that describe Jose's interests. Enter the words in the paragraph below.

```
S  E  L  T  E  C  H  N  I  C  A  L  U  C  E  M  T  U  C  P
G  C  P  A  M  R  E  R  T  E  R  T  M  R  A  M  T  R  W  T
S  O  F  T  W  A  R  E  C  O  N  I  G  L  W  T  U  C  T  F
W  M  T  T  M  N  L  R  R  C  O  D  E  R  S  C  M  O  F  S
S  P  R  O  G  R  A  M  M  E  R  R  R  A  I  U  A  M  S  M
G  U  E  O  A  N  C  R  R  O  P  E  M  P  G  R  O  A  U  C
F  T  A  M  M  T  E  R  T  C  T  R  C  P  S  O  E  W  F  O
R  E  U  P  E  C  O  A  D  E  S  T  F  M  A  C  E  O  O  S
A  R  A  E  R  L  P  G  C  M  T  E  T  M  R  E  R  A  S  T
G  P  T  T  M  R  R  W  O  S  E  O  O  O  R  F  E  U  M  T
```

Jose loves anything _ _ _ _ _ _ _ _ _. He learnt how to use a _

_ _ _ _ _ _ _ better than his parents and before he could

walk, and in record speed learnt how to become a _ _ _ _ _

_ _ _ _ _ _ _ _ _ _ _ _. As he grew up, he started his own

YouTube channel for other _ _ _ _ _ _ and he loves being a _

_ _ _ _.

CHAPTER 3. RAVENHALL MANOR

The hallway was bustling with activity, and it was a bit overwhelming. New people, new surroundings - it was all a bit much to take in at once. But at the same time, there was a sense of excitement in the air, a feeling of adventure waiting just around the corner.

You stood there with the other kids, suitcases, and backpacks at our feet, looking around for any sign of the grown-ups. But the hallway was eerily quiet - the only sound was the soft rustle of leaves outside.

Ethan, ever the artist, had decided to sketch the hallway in his notepad. But as he looked down at his work, a look of confusion crossed his face. "Wait a minute," he said. "I feel like I'm missing something..."

Puzzle 8: Spot the difference

Ethan decided to sketch the hallway upside down in his notepad. He did not capture one thing though - can you tell what he missed out?

As you were waiting, your eyes scanned the room, taking in every detail. And then, like a beacon in the darkness, you spotted it - a coffee table book sitting on a nearby table. It was the guest book, and as you flipped through its pages, you found an introduction written up that gives you a glimpse into the history of Ravenhall Manor.

Puzzle 9: Book with missing words

Solve the following puzzle based on the clues given. Then enter the words in the Ravenhall Manor guest book.

Across

[2] Related to the field of medicine
[6] People who use words to create stories
[7] Place where people receive medical care

Down

[1] Get and education and live there at the same time
[3] Not occupied or filled
[4] People who paint or sketches
[5] Members of the armed forces

Ravenhall Manor has a long and storied history, dating back several hundred years. Originally built as a grand country estate, the manor has been home to many notable figures throughout the years, from wealthy aristocrats to famous _ _ _ _ _ _ _ and _ _ _ _ _ _ _.

During the Second World War, Ravenhall Manor was repurposed as a _ _ _ _ _ _ _ _ for wounded _ _ _ _ _ _ _ _ _. The grand halls and spacious rooms were filled with cots and _ _ _ _ _ _ _ equipment, and the sound of nurses' footsteps echoed through the halls day and night. Many brave men and women were treated at Ravenhall, and countless lives were saved within its walls.

After the war, Ravenhall Manor was left _ _ _ _ _ for many years, its grandeur fading and its walls falling into disrepair. But in recent years, a group of dedicated individuals have worked tirelessly to restore the manor to its former glory.

Today, Ravenhall Manor is a thriving _ _ _ _ _ _ _ _ _ _ _ _ _ _ for young children from all over the world. Its winding corridors and the history of the manor adds a certain sense of intrigue and wonder to every activity and lesson.

During the summer months, the manor is empty, its grand halls and sprawling grounds silent and still. The teachers and staff take a well-deserved break, and the only sounds that can be heard are the chirping of birds and the rustling of leaves in the breeze.

It was a riveting read, delving into the history of Ravenhall Manor. Eva, ever the intrepid explorer, turned the handle of the old wooden door. It let out a loud creak, protesting being disturbed from its long slumber. But what lay behind was worth the disturbance - a vast library, with towering bookcases lining the walls and old volumes piled high on tables and desks. The smell of old parchment and leather-bound books filled the air, and it was easy to get lost in the enchantment of it all.

The discovery of the library left us all in a state of wonder. The walls were lined with shelves of ancient books, their spines worn and their pages yellowed with age. The smell of musty paper hung in the air, and the creaking of the floorboards beneath our feet added to the atmosphere of antiquity.

But the most intriguing part of the room was a glass cabinet filled with World War artefacts - gas masks, helmets, and other military paraphernalia. It was as if we had stepped back in time, and the ghosts of soldiers long gone were whispering their stories in our ears.

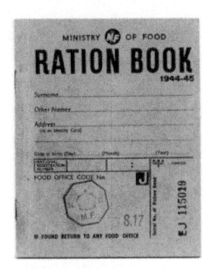

Puzzle 10. Spot the difference

Puzzle 11. What did you do?

As you take in the surroundings, a rush of adventure bubbles up within you, causing you to wander around the room. Penny and Eva can be seen with their noses buried in the old dusty books, while Ethan and Oskar are engrossed in examining the artefacts in the glass cabinet. Just as you take a step forward, your foot slips, causing you to stumble and tumble to the ground. What just happened? Find the difference between the two photos.

Something happened when you fell onto the item missing in the photo. A sudden creaking noise caught everyone's attention. It seemed to come from the other side of the room, and you all turned to see what it was. To your amazement, a hidden door had opened in the bookshelf, revealing a secret room beyond.

A voice from the other side of the hidden door could be heard.

"What took you so long?"

CHAPTER 4. THE TEACHERS

As Oskar, Eva, Penny, Ethan, Jose, and you peered through the secret door, your sense of adventure mingled with apprehension. Two grown-ups, a man and a younger woman, stood inside the room, their gazes locked on you all. The man spoke up, his voice warm and welcoming. "Come in, we don't bite," he said with a chuckle. "I'm Mr. Williams, one of your teachers. And this is Miss Green," he continued, pointing to the younger woman who stood beside him, her demeanour aloof and dour.

Despite her stern appearance, Miss Green's eyes flickered with curiosity as she observed the group of young spies-in-training. You couldn't help but feel a bit intimidated by her presence, but also intrigued by what secrets she might be keeping.

As you stepped inside the room, Mr. Williams continued his introductions. "Now, I'm sure you're all wondering why you've been invited to Ravenhall Manor. It's because you have been selected for a very special mission," he explained, a glint of excitement in his eye. "And we are here to help train you to be the best young spies you can be."

"You'll be spending the next week here, and during that time, we'll be teaching you the basics of secret messaging, code breaking, and stealth. But first, it's important that you get to know each other and explore the manor's many secrets."

Miss Green stood quietly by his side, showing no emotions. "We'll be watching your progress closely," she added in a stern tone. "Only the best will be selected to continue on to more advanced training."

Mr. Williams shot her a warning look before turning back to the young spies with a smile. "But don't worry, it's all in good fun. Are you up for the challenge?" he asked, his eyes twinkling.

"YES!" everyone said, barely containing their enthusiasm.

Mr. Williams cleared his throat and continued, "Now, let's talk about what makes a good spy agent. It's not just about being able to run fast or jump high. It's about having sharp eyes and ears, being able to blend in and observe without being noticed. It's about being able to think on your feet, to solve problems quickly and creatively. And most importantly, it's about being able to keep a secret, to never reveal your true identity or mission, even under the most trying circumstances.

"Let's test your observational skills first. Both myself and Miss Green have been in the field and been active spies. What are our skills?

Puzzle 12. Mr Williams

Match the words from the following list and discover Mr Williams' skills as a spy:

_____ 1. Undercover	A. Secret
_____ 2. Sharp eye	B. Speaking
_____ 3. Questions	C. Covering
_____ 4. Languages	D. Queries
_____ 5. Hiding	E. Fit in
_____ 6. Blend in	F. Detail

Use the words to the <u>left</u> to fill in the blanks in the paragraph below.

Mr. Williams had a reputation for being an expert in

_ _ _ _ _ _ _ _ _ _ work. He had a _ _ _ _ _ _ _ _ for detail and was able to pick up on even the slightest hints of suspicious activity. He was also great at asking tough _ _ _ _ _ _ _ _ _, able to extract valuable information from even the most stubborn of sources.

In addition, Mr. Williams was also fluent in several _ _ _ _ _ _ _ _ _, as he has travelled to many countries and met with local people. Furthermore, Mr. Williams was also an expert in the art of _ _ _ _ _ _ in plain sight. He knew how to change his appearance and mannerisms to _ _ _ _ _ _ _ with any crowd.

Puzzle 13. Miss Green

Find the hidden words in the word search and complete the sentences.

```
            A A B E J A T A
            O C R K R N E C A A
          A R R S E K O R J U D O
        D N E T W O R K K K U C E T
      S A A T A R T S E O O C N R O A
      E K A S T E R T T C O W A C O E
  B N N O C A C K B W U R H K J W E T
  A C K S K C T A T T K H A T R R E R
  C R H A C R W R D S R A K H O A O W
  A M A C N C R A E A R C T J T K C A
  N W T B T A A T O B A C C E O E E K
    O C B N E J E A O T E J S O K D
    O D C C A T C C K S S K T E A O
      A H H A C K E R T S R T C D
      E S O R O A N T T E K S C O
        D E C M A S E N S J A E
        K U A B K A E C T A U K
          T J A E D K O W E C
          A T E K H E N R
            T T E K E C
            C O M T M O
            K C C C
```

Words List

karate	judo	combat	hacker
network	access		

Miss Green is a master of several different forms of martial arts, including _ _ _ _ _ _, _ _ _ _ , and taekwondo. In addition to these more traditional forms of martial arts, Miss Green has also studied a variety of modern combative systems, such as Krav Maga and Brazilian Jiu-Jitsu. These disciplines have allowed her to develop a well-rounded skill set that includes grappling, striking, and ground _ _ _ _ _ _ techniques. In addition to her physical and tactical skills, Miss Green was also an accomplished _ _ _ _ _ _ and computer expert. She had spent many years working in the field of cyber espionage, using her skills to infiltrate enemy computer _ _ _ _ _ _ _ and gather valuable intelligence. She is skilled at identifying and exploiting vulnerabilities in computer systems, and can often gain _ _ _ _ _ _ to even the most heavily guarded networks.

As Mr. Williams was finishing up, there was a loud knocking at the door, followed by the sound of a key turning in the lock. The door opened to reveal the headmaster, Mr. Long, looking sour and uncomfortable. "What are all of you doing here?" he demanded, his gaze flickering disapprovingly over the group of young spies-in-training. "This is the summer term, you know. I didn't expect to find anyone here."

Mr. Williams stepped forward, his voice calm and even. "As you know, Mr. Long, Ravenhall Manor is owned by the government. During the summer months, the building is used for our own purposes. These students have been invited to attend our special summer school."

Mr. Long's expression softened slightly, but he still looked uncomfortable. "Very well," he said, before turning on his heel and making a hasty exit.

Puzzle 14. Mr Long

Find out more about Mr Long. Match the words from the following list.

H		D	M		S	T		R	Principal
L		N		L	Y				Alone
T			C	H		R			Educator
H		S	T		R	Y			Back in time
C		L	L		C	T		R	Keeper
P		B	L		C	S	P		K	R	Presenter

Use the words to the **left** to fill in the blanks in the paragraph below.

Mr Long is the _ _ _ _ _ _ _ _ _ _ _ of Ravenhall Manor. He is known for being a somewhat _ _ _ _ _ _ figure, rarely being social or speaking with the students or staff unless it is absolutely necessary.

To the outside world, Mr. Long is seen as a respected _ _ _ _ _ _ _ and academic, with a deep knowledge of _ _ _ _ _ _ _ and a passion for education.

His knowledge of World War I and II has made him a keen _ _ _ _ _ _ _ _ of wartime memorabilia such as medals and other artefacts. He is well-regarded in the academic community, and is often invited as a _ _ _ _ _ _ _ _ _ _ _ _ _ at conferences and other events.

Mr. Williams offered a sincere apology for the abrupt interruption, acknowledging that it had probably been a long and overwhelming day for us. With a warm smile, he encouraged us to make our way to our living quarters to settle in before the evening's dinner.

"Take some time to explore and get comfortable," he suggested. "We'll reconvene later this evening for dinner and further instruction. Remember, we're all in this together. Let's make the most of this opportunity and learn all that we can."

You and the others get shown to your living quarters by Miss Green. We are all sleeping in the same hall, so hopefully no one snores! The bed looked inviting but although you might be tired, you all head to the dining room.

For dinner, you and the others have the best spaghetti Bolognese you have ever tasted. It was warm, filling and comforting, which was perfect, as you were a bit nervous and restless about staying over.

As night fell, the dorm room was filled with a cacophony of sounds - the rhythmic snoring of Jose and the calming whale noises of Eva's phone. You lay in bed, trying to drift off to sleep but finding it difficult with the noise. Just as you were about to give up, a strange feeling washed over you. It was as if you were in a dream-like state, yet fully awake.

As you gazed out the window, the night sky was eerily still. It was then that you noticed the faint glow of the lighthouse in the distance. Was it really on, or just a figment of your imagination?

CHAPTER 5. SECRET MESSAGES IN MORSE CODE

You burst into the secret room in the library, feeling a bit frazzled from oversleeping. As you enter, you see Oskar sitting down, surrounded by your new friends with Mr Williams at the front of the room, poised and ready to start the lesson. Miss Green is standing at the back of the room, looking aloof and distant. Not a hint of a smile on her face.

"Good morning" , Mr Williams said. " I trust you had a restful night's sleep and are now feeling well-rested and settled in. In the coming days, we shall delve into the fascinating world of code-making, code-breaking, and the art of secret messaging. You will learn the origins and history of codes, as well as the various methods and techniques employed to create and decipher them."

You take the seat next to Oskar and glance over to your left. Ethan is sitting on the other side with a huge smile on his face, like the Cheshire cat from Alice in Wonderland!

Mr Williams continues. "So let's begin. Throughout history, secret messages have been used to pass on important information between people. In ancient times, the Greeks used a type of code called scytale, where they would wrap messages around a rod and only the recipient with a rod of the same size could read it.

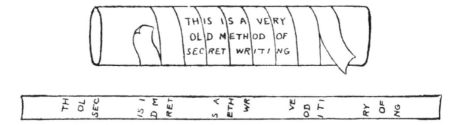

"During the Renaissance period, codes were used to protect important letters and to keep secret the conversations of diplomats. Mary Queen of Scots famously used a cipher to communicate with her conspirators before she was imprisoned."

"A hundred years ago, during World War II, secret codes and ciphers were more important than ever before. In this war, there were two groups fighting against each other - the Allies and the Germans. Both sides wanted to send messages to their own people, but they didn't want the other side to understand what they were saying. What famous code was used, do you think?"

"Oh, I know!" said Ethan excitedly. "It's morse code. I think I am related to Samuel Morse, the inventor of the code in the 1880s. It was a way of sending messages over long distances before phones and computers were invented. How cool is that?!"

"That would be a great family connection, Ethan", Mr Williams said. "You are absolutely right, the Allies used Morse code to send messages across long distances, without the enemy knowing what was being said."

"The message could be written down, as dots and dashes, and sent via carrier pigeon. Most common method was using the telegraph to send the message. Can anyone tell me what a telegraph is?"

Oskar raised his hand. "It's like a long-wired phone but instead of hearing a voice, you could only hear a clicking noise from one place to another. The sender of the message would use the key to tap out the message and the receiver would hear the clicking noise."

"That's right, Oskar", said Mr Williams. "So the morse code, which consists of 'dots' and 'dashes' would make short and long clicking noises."

Miss Green was now handing out a sheet of paper. She was still not smiling.

Mr Williams said: "When you want to write a message using Morse code, you need to think about what letters and numbers you want to use, and then look up the dots and dashes that represent each letter or number. Miss Green has just handed out the whole alphabet in morse code"

International Morse Code

1. The length of a dot is one unit.
2. A dash is three units.
3. The space between parts of the same letter is one unit.
4. The space between letters is three units.
5. The space between words is seven units.

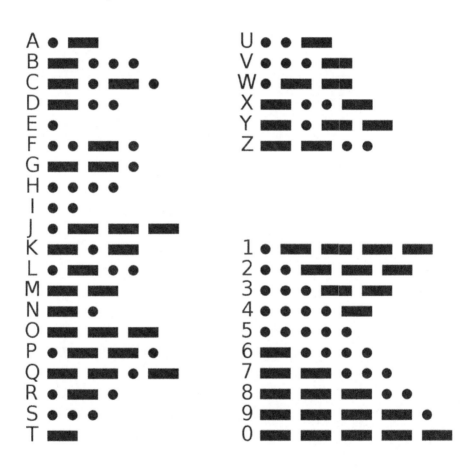

Mr Williams went up to the whiteboard and started to write a dot and a dash.

"Each letter of the alphabet, as well as numbers and some punctuation marks, is represented by a unique combination of dots and dashes.

For instance, the letter "A" is represented by a single dot followed by a dash:

.-

while the letter "B" is represented by a dash followed by three dots:

-...

Once you know the dots and dashes for each letter or number, you can start writing your message in Morse code by using dots and dashes to represent each letter or number. You can use a pen and paper or even tap the dots and dashes out using your fingers or a tool like a flashlight."

"Let's write a message together. Let's write HELLO WORLD"

Use / to show that's the end of the code for the letter. So HELLO is:

..../ . /.-.. /.-../ --- /

And WORLD would be (write your answer):

Puzzle 15. Write a message in morse code

Let's practise! Write "This is a secret message" in morse code.

"OK, so we have written a message. Let's try to **decode** a message. Use the sheet to help you decode."

MORSE CODE
(CODE ORDER)

E	•		T	—
I	• •		M	— —
S	• • •		O	— — —
H	• • • •		N	— •
A	• —		G	— — •
U	• • —		Z	— — • •
V	• • • —		Q	— — • —
W	• — —		D	— • •
J	• — — —		B	— • • •
R	• — •		K	— • —
L	• — • •		C	— • — •
F	• • — •		Y	— • — —
P	• — — •		X	— • • —
1	• — — — —		6	— • • • •
2	• • — — —		7	— — • • •
3	• • • — —		8	— — — • •
4	• • • • —		9	— — — — •
5	• • • • •		0	— — — — —

Can you guess what the following code says?

..../ . / .-.. / .-../ --- /

..../ --- / .-- /

.- / .-./ . /

-.--/ ---/ ..- /

That's right! It says "Hello, how are you?"

Puzzle 16. Decipher a secret message in morse code

.- / ... /

.- /

.../ .--./ -.--/

-/ ..../ ./

.---/ ---/ -.../

../ .../

-./ ---/ -/

-/ ---/

--./. /-/

-.-./ .- /..- /--. /..../ -

As the day progressed, your mind was consumed with thoughts of dots and dashes. Even during bushcraft, as you worked to build a shelter and start a fire, you found yourself mentally reciting the code in a bid to commit it to memory.

The afternoon wore on and the teachers surprised the group with piping hot pizzas, loaded with all your favourite toppings. The delicious aroma filled the air, tempting even the most health-conscious among you to indulge in the cheesy, gooey goodness.

As you savoured each bite, Ethan's enthusiasm for secret codes and spying during the world wars kept you all engaged, his words sparking your imagination and inspiring new ideas.

But as the night crept in, exhaustion overtook you. Excusing yourself from the lively chatter of your friends, you retreated to your bedroom, the comfort of your bed beckoning. Lying down, your thoughts drifted to your family, and the warm memories of home brought a sense of comfort and peace.

Soon, you drifted into a deep sleep, lost in a world of dreams. Not even the sounds of the thunder and lightning outside could rouse you from your slumber.

CHAPTER 6. PIGPEN CIPHER

"Ah what a beautiful day!" Mr Williams joyfully exclaimed as he entered the room. Today, I'm about to take you on an amazing journey to discover this fantastic secret code that's been around for hundreds of years!"

Mr Williams' enthusiasm was infectious, and his lessons never felt boring. You look around and see the others hanging to his every word.

"Once upon a time, back in the 18th century, there were these known secret societies. One of them was called the Freemasons. They were a group of skilled craftsmen and builders who had lots of secrets. They used special handshakes, rituals, and symbols to recognise each other, and they needed a way to keep their secrets safe. They came up with a sneaky way to write secret messages using a code called the Pigpen Cipher. Now, you might be wondering why it's called the "Pigpen" Cipher. It's because the way the code is written looks like the little pens where farmers keep their pigs."

"So, how does the Pigpen Cipher work? It's actually pretty simple and easy to learn. First, imagine two tic-tac-toe grids and two X-shaped grids. That's right, just like the games you've played with your friends!"

Mr Williams turned to the whiteboard and drew up the grids.

"Now, we're going to put the alphabet inside these grids. In the first tic-tac-toe grid, you'll write the letters A to I, one letter in each box. Like this:"

"Next, you'll fill in the second tic-tac-toe grid with the letters J to R, as well as place a dot in each grid:"

"And now, we're going to fill in the two X-shaped grids. The first X-shaped grid will have the letters S to V:"

"And finally the last letters of the alphabet:"

"To write a message using the Pigpen Cipher, you just need to replace each letter with the part of the grid it's in. For example, if you wanted to write the letter A, you would draw the lines that surround A in the grid like this:"

"The letter B is surrounded by three lines in the top-middle part so it would look like this:"

"And so on for the rest of the alphabet."

"Let's try writing a secret message together! How about the word "HELLO"? "

"First, we'll find the letter H in the first tic-tac-toe grid. It's in the bottom-middle part and we draw the lines that surround H."

"Next is E, which is in the middle of the first grid, so we'll draw a square:"

"For L, we'll draw the top-right corner of the second grid with a dot: "

"Finally, we'll find O in the middle-right of the second grid and draw three lines and a dot like this:"

"So our secret message looks like this: "

Here's the full pigpen cipher:

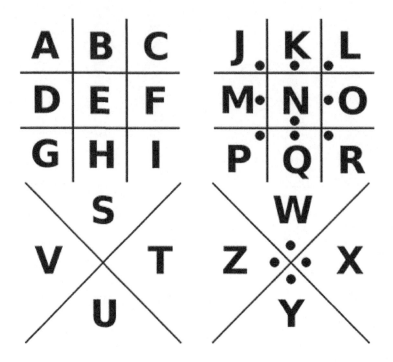

Puzzle 17. Decipher pigpen coded message

Let's practise. Can you decode the following message?

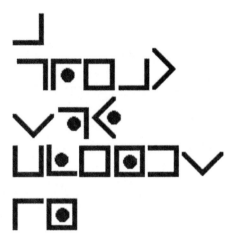

Puzzle 18. Write a pigpen coded message

Now write the following message in pigpen:

X marks the spot

Puzzle 19: Taking a break

Eva rushed out of the room, like her pants were on fire. "What is wrong with her?" you asked. "Too many juice boxes" said Oskar. "I guess she was in a hurry to use the restroom." Help Eva find her way down the stairs. Start at "S" (at the top of the stairs) and finish at "E" (bottom corner of the stairs).

As we gathered our things and prepared to leave, a loud crash echoed through the hallway, sending everyone's eyes darting towards the door. Even Mr. Williams, usually composed and unflappable, quickened his pace towards the source of the disturbance. Before he could lay a hand on the doorknob, however, it was flung open from the other side, revealing the stern figure of Headmaster Long.

In his grasp, he held onto the collar of a poor Eva, her eyes downcast and her demeanour cowed by the force of his presence. With a raised and heated tone, he accused her of tripping him up on purpose.

Though Eva stammered out an apology, her words were lost amidst the tumult of the headmaster's rage. You couldn't stand the way he was treating her, and you felt a surge of anger rise up within you. Thankfully, Miss Green intervened before things could escalate any further. With a firm but gentle touch, she pried Eva free from the headmaster's grasp, her voice ringing out in a soothing tone that calmed down the tense atmosphere.

"Perhaps Eva can be a bit clumsy at times," she said, "but she had our permission to use the facilities. There was no harm done."

Mr. Long begrudgingly relented, his dark cloud of anger dissipating as he turned to leave. But you knew that this wouldn't be the last time he would try to make life difficult for Eva and the rest of your friends. And that realisation left a sour taste in your mouth, as you wondered what other challenges lay ahead.

CHAPTER 7. SUBSTITUTING LETTERS

The next day, the morning sun peeked through the windows, casting a warm glow across the classroom. The tension from yesterday seemed to have dissipated, and we all felt more at ease. It was reassuring to know that the teachers had our backs, and we were determined to stay out of Headmaster Long's way.

Miss Green still looked serious, but I could sense that she was no longer as harsh as before. Mr. Williams, on the other hand, was brimming with energy as always. He wasted no time in getting us started on our new lesson for the day.

"Good morning, children! Today, we are going to learn a super cool way to send secret messages to your friends. It's called letter substitution, and it's a sneaky but clever way to keep your messages hidden from prying eyes."

"The idea is to replace each letter in the message with a different letter, according to a secret key that you and your friend both know. This makes the message look like gibberish to anyone who doesn't know the key, but easy to read for those who do!"

"One of the most famous substitution ciphers is the Caesar Cipher, named after Julius Caesar, a famous Roman general and politician who lived more than 2,000 years ago. Julius Caesar used this cipher to send secret messages to his generals during his many battles and conquests. In the Middle Ages, the Caesar cipher was commonly used by European kings and queens and their courts to communicate in secret. The cipher was also used by military leaders and diplomats to send messages that could not be easily deciphered by enemy spies."

"So how does it work? The Caesar cipher works by replacing each letter in his message with a letter that was a certain number of positions later in the alphabet. "

"For example, if we use a "shift" of 3, the letter A would become D, B would become E, and so on. The letter "Z" wraps around to the beginning of the alphabet, so if the shift is 3, "Z" becomes "C"."

Miss Green hands everyone a circular disc with the letters on. It has two layers, with the top layer being a smaller circle that rotates around a larger fixed bottom layer. The top layer has cutouts of the 26 letters of the alphabet, arranged in a clockwise order. As you rotate the top layer, you can feel the slight resistance and hear a soft clicking sound as the letters slot into place.

(At the back of the book, you can cut out your own Caesar cipher.)

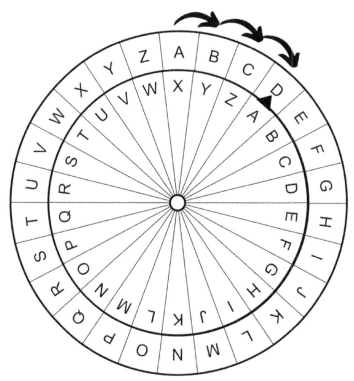

For a shift of "3" move the inner wheel 3 steps.
The letters on the inner wheel should be replaced
by the letter on the outer wheel

"Let's see how this works with a real example. Imagine you want to send your friend the message "HELLO". Using a Caesar Cipher with a shift of 3, you would replace each letter with the letter that comes three positions later in the alphabet:"

H -> K
E -> H
L -> O
L -> O
O -> R

"So, your secret message would be "KHOOR"! Pretty cool, right?

"To decode the message, your friend would do the reverse: replace each letter with the letter that comes three positions earlier in the alphabet:"

K -> H
H -> E
O -> L
O -> L
R -> O

"And just like that, your friend would be able to read your secret message: "HELLO"!

If you don't have a disc, or you rather use pen and paper, you can use the following table to track which letter has been substituted."

A	B	C	D	E	F	G	H	I	J	K	L	M	N	O	P	Q	R	S	T	U	V	W	X	Y	Z

Puzzle 20. Use Caesar cipher to create a message

Write down the following message and encrypt using a shift of 10.

The spymaster is the leader of spies

Puzzle 21. Decode using Caesar cipher

What does this say?

Ugvw tjwscafy ak s yggv kcadd xgj s khq lg zsnw

"Now, you might be thinking, "But what if someone figures out the shift we're using?" That's a great point! The Caesar Cipher is easy to crack if someone knows that you're using it. If you can figure out one letter, you can understand the number of shifts being used, and decode the rest of the message."

"Is there a way to make it harder?" asked Penny.

"Yes, there is. You can make random substitutions. Replace each letter with a different letter or a symbol. For example, you could replace the letter "A" with the symbol "*". This will make it much harder to guess."

"To use a cipher, you and the person you're sending the message to both need to know the rules for how to change the letters in your message. You can write down the rules and share them with the person you're sending the message to, or you can come up with your own secret rules that only the two of you know."

CHAPTER 8. AN ACCIDENT HAPPENS

During a break, the young spy agents decided to explore the library, with its towering bookshelves filled with ancient volumes and secret passages. Oskar, a keen collector of antiques, was particularly drawn to the display and couldn't resist opening the glass cabinet, revealing a treasure trove of artefacts just waiting to be touched.

"Oh!" exclaimed Oskar, "the cabinet door is open." With a gentle click, the group began examining the fascinating objects inside. However, you couldn't help but feel a sense of unease and warned Oskar to be careful.

Despite your warning, Oskar couldn't resist taking a closer look and reached for an old compass. Suddenly, there was a loud noise, and the compass slipped from Oskar's grasp, crashing to the ground. As the group rushed over to investigate, they noticed an aged piece of paper folded and stuck inside the compass.

Ethan eagerly picked up the paper, we huddled around him and the paper to study it closely. The yellowed paper had a rough texture, as if it had been passed from hand to hand over the years. The writing was faded, but still legible. It appeared to be a coded message, and the group knew they had stumbled upon something important.

Puzzle 22. Secret message

The yellow paper showed a map and something else on the back of it:

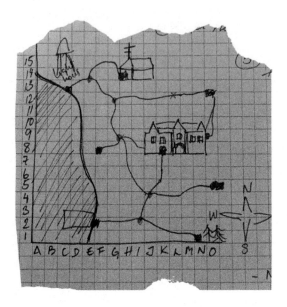

Gwc kiv pqlm gwcz bzmiaczma qv bpm

cvlmzozwcvl bcvvmta

Dqsbwz Tivom

You could feel the excitement in the air as we huddled around the secret message and map. It was like we had stumbled upon a treasure map. The thought of hidden treasures in underground tunnels was intriguing. Suddenly, the realisation hit us that we didn't know where we were on the map. We needed to figure out our location before we could find the treasure.

All six of us were talking at once, and no one was listening. Suddenly, a sharp whistling sound pierced the air. It was Oskar, now standing on a chair, trying to take control of the situation.

"Guys, we must work together if we are going to do something with this map. Let's take a step at a time. First, who wants to explore the map and find the tunnels and the treasure?"

All of us raised our hands.

"OK," Oskar said. "Let's explore. But we can't risk being caught by the headmaster, or we may get kicked out of school early. Let's do this at night, when everyone is asleep."

Jose chimed in, "I can make headlights for all of us so we can still see in the dark." Everyone nodded in approval.

Penny asked, "Shouldn't we tell Miss Green and Mr Williams?" Oskar took a minute to think before responding. "What if this is a test from them? Maybe we are meant to have found this map and to explore. Like we did the first day here when we found the secret door and the classroom?"

We agreed to keep it between us for now.

CHAPTER 9. UNDERGROUND TUNNELS

At 10pm that night, we left our bedrooms and quietly started to look for openings in the walls where we could find the start of our underground tunnels. The dim glow of Jose's homemade headlights illuminated the way as we tiptoed down the darkened corridors, our hearts pounding with excitement and fear.

As we were exploring the Manor, Penny noticed that there was a bookshelf in the living room area that looked a bit strange. Upon closer inspection, the books were arranged in a specific order, and there was a small gap at the bottom of the shelf that looked like it might be an opening. We managed to push the bookshelf aside, revealing a small room with a spiral staircase leading down. At the bottom, we found themselves in a dark tunnel, with only our headlights to guide the way.

Puzzle 23. Explore the tunnels

Let's look at the map again. We can see the Manor on the map but there seems to be three ways from the mansion to the tunnels.

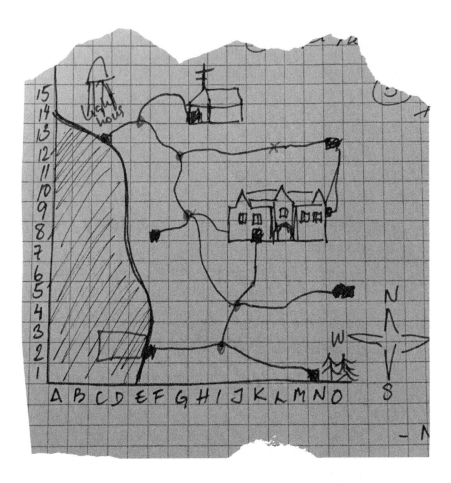

Whilst exploring the tunnels, you come across these messages on the wall. They seem familiar - do you remember what they are?

Let's decipher the messages - and figure out which wall is linked to the coordinates on the map.

Map position: J 4

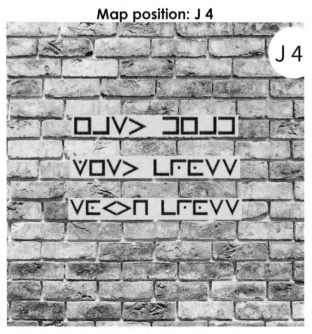

Map position: E 13

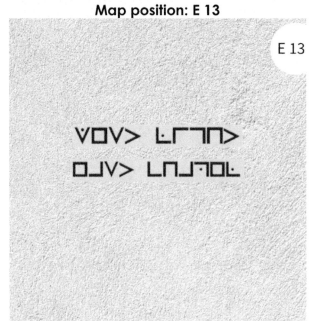

Map position: G 12

Map position: G 9

Map position: 1 2

The messages on the walls gave us more clues on where we can find other places. Where could the treasure be? Let's map out the place with the coordinates on the map.

Map position: The Chapel

Coordinates: _____

Map position: The Jetty **Coordinates:** _____

Map position: The Lighthouse **Coordinates:** _____

Map position: The Woods **Coordinates:** _____

Map position: A Dead End **Coordinates:** _____

Map position: Another Dead End **Coordinates:** _____

Map position: The Treasure Room Coordinates: _____

As we entered the treasure room, our eyes widened with wonder and amazement. It was like stepping into a treasure trove, filled with an abundance of priceless artefacts and antiques. The walls were adorned with paintings that depicted scenes from a time long past. Oskar's eyes gleamed as he examined the items. "These items are from the World Wars," he exclaimed, "Just the paintings alone could fetch a fortune!"

What had we stumbled upon?

CHAPTER 10. WHAT DID WE FIND?

As Penny looked at the items on the antique desk, her eyes fell upon a fragile, yellowed paper that immediately caught her attention. Upon closer inspection, she realised that it was an old letter, still in remarkably good condition. Excitedly, she motioned for you to come closer and read it with her. As you both peered over the page, she began to read the words out loud, her voice trembling with anticipation as the others gathered around to listen in.

My dear grandson

I want to share with you a secret that may become useful for you. When I was wounded during the war, the hospital I was at (which is now

---

> *known as Ravenhall Manor) have underground tunnels.*
>
> *I used to be part of a smuggling gang that imported weapons and ammunition to German spies in Britain. Although the war is over, I am sure that you will find the tunnels as useful as I did.*
>
> *Your dearest*
>
> *V.L.*

Penny's hand trembled as she held the letter, her eyes scanning the words carefully. Who was V.L.? It had to be Viktor Lange, the same name on the back of the map. But why did the name sound familiar?

Oskar spoke up, his voice laced with excitement. "I have a theory, but it might sound a bit mad," he said, drawing everyone's attention. "You see, my name is spelled with a 'k' instead of a 'c'." Before anyone could ask what that had to do with anything, Ethan suddenly interrupted. "Can you all see that light?" he exclaimed. They turned to look, and sure enough, there was a flickering light in the distance, rhythmic and constant. But where did it come from? It didn't seem to be coming from the ceiling, and the lightbulb in the room was intact. As they puzzled over this, a realisation hit you.

You had seen that same flickering light several times at night. "I think I know what that light is," you said slowly. "It's from the lighthouse. They've been flashing the light ever since we got here. Could it be that someone is communicating by morse code using the lighthouse?"

Puzzle 24. Mysterious lights

Let's see if your theory is correct. Solve the following morse code

.. / -./ -.-./ ---/ --/ ../ -./ --
./

.-/ -/

--/ ../ -../ -. /../ --./ ..../ -
/

-.../ . /

.-./ ./ .-/ -../ -.--/

"That's literally in the next few minutes," Jose remarked. Oskar took charge, trying to make sense of the situation. "Who sent that message? They must be messaging someone at the school, so someone is meeting up with them. The items in this room are of high value, and they are hidden for a reason, I bet," he stated.

You suggested informing Mr. Williams and Miss Green, but Eva raised a valid concern: what if they were involved?

"Good point. We can contact my uncle Gavin on my mobile. I can't get any reception here." Oskar said, waving his phone in the air as if that would help.

"We're not far from the Manor" said Eva. She had taken upon herself to be the map reader. "I'm happy to go somewhere where we can find reception so we can call for help. Can someone come with me though?" Jose volunteered to and they both set off towards the manor.

"That leaves the four of us to find out who these people are, and who they are here to meet. They must be coming in from the sea, don't you think?", said Penny thoughtfully.

Oskar suggested splitting up to get a better chance of figuring out who these mysterious people were and why they were meeting at the manor. "We can have two of us hiding in the antique wardrobe in the corner in case they come here," he said, "while the other two go to the coastline."

You spoke up and volunteered to go to the coastline, not wanting to be stuck in a cramped wardrobe. Penny immediately offered to join you, saying she preferred the fresh air. Time was running out, as it was almost midnight.

With our hearts beating fast, we went back into the tunnels and made our way quickly to the jetty. We stopped and decided to wait behind some well-placed bushes with a good vantage point overlooking the calm sea. It was now very dark as we turned off Jose's home-made headlights. The howling of the owl in the forest added an extra layer of tension to the already tense situation. We waited in silence, trying to catch any sign of movement on the water.

And then there it was. A boat. A rowing boat, with three silhouettes. The sound of the oars dipping into the water filled the air, and you started to wonder if hiding in the antique wardrobe might have been a safer choice.

CHAPTER 11. CONCLUSION

As the figures disembarked from the boat and stepped onto the jetty, we strained our eyes to try to make out their faces, but they remained shrouded in darkness. Three grown men, possibly dangerous, had arrived on the island.

But then, to our surprise, a fourth voice joined the group. It occurred to me that perhaps they weren't meeting someone in the treasure room after all, but rather they were meeting someone at the jetty. My heart pounding, I turned to Penny and saw the same fear as I had etched on her face. We both knew that we had to stay hidden and observe their actions, to try and figure out what was really going on.

Puzzle 25. Who is it?

Mr Williams, Miss Green or Mr Long? Or someone else?
Unscramble the following list of shuffled words to meaningful
words! Then enter the letters in the grey boxes in the grid
below.

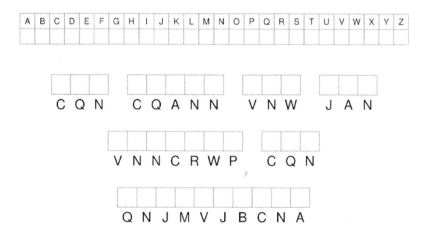

A	B	C	D	E	F	G	H	I	J	K	L	M	N	O	P	Q	R	S	T	U	V	W	X	Y	Z

C Q N   C Q A N N   V N W   J A N

V N N C R W P   C Q N

Q N J M V J B C N A

Realisation dawned upon us as we understood why the headmaster was so unhappy about us being there. Perhaps he thought he could operate freely without anyone around during the summer. But instead, he had us, young spies-in-training, wandering around and investigating. It was clear now why he was scared of being discovered.

However, we were now in a dilemma. We knew who the three men were meeting, but we didn't know if they were involved in any criminal activity. We were crouching behind the bushes in the dark, with potentially dangerous individuals. How would we get out of this?

Suddenly, a stern and serious voice boomed through the air: "Hands up!" You recognised it as Miss Green's voice. Peering out of the bushes, you saw both Miss Green and Mr Williams standing there, guns pointed at the four individuals on the jetty. You let out a sigh of relief as you saw the police officers rushing towards them from the lawn, along with Oskar and the rest of your friends. You stood up and were grateful to be out of harm's way.

Puzzle 24. To the rescue

Someone else turns up apart from the teachers. Can you figure out who it is?

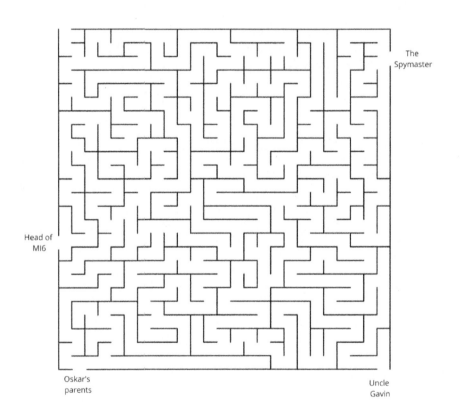

Following a restful night's sleep and a lazy lie-in, we reconvened with our teachers and Uncle Gavin at the dining hall for breakfast. "Good morning, bright stars!" boomed Mr. Williams in his usual energetic voice. Despite our well-rested state, we were still a bit groggy and uncertain about the events of the previous night. Sensing our confusion, Mr. Williams showed us a newspaper to bring us up to speed.

It all started to make sense now - the war artefacts found in the treasure room, the secret tunnels, and the strange behaviour of the headmaster. We had stumbled upon a smuggling ring! The headmaster, Victor Long, was the grandson of a German spy named Viktor Lange who had uncovered the tunnels during the war. But instead of becoming a war hero, Lange became bitter and passed his resentment to his grandson who grew up to be the leader of a gang of treasure hunters involved in heists worth millions of dollars around the world.

Uncle Gavin, looking serious, turned to us and reminded us that being a spy meant keeping secrets. We couldn't tell anyone about our involvement in foiling this international smuggling ring. If we did, we would be risking our own and our families' lives. But he also congratulated us on our accomplishment and invited us to MI6 in London where we would be celebrated and recognised for our bravery.

We felt proud and honoured to have been a part of such a big mission. It was a huge accomplishment, and we were grateful to have the opportunity to work with such amazing mentors. We knew that we still had a lot to learn, but we were excited to continue on this path and become helpful assets for the team.

**Congratulations on finishing
The Ravenhall Manor Mystery.**

More Oskar & Friends stories are coming!

HINTS

Puzzle 1

Read each word backwards

Puzzle 2

A British agency, normally referred to as MI6

S_ _ _ _ _ _   I_ _ _ _ _ _ _ _ _ _   E S_ _ _ _ _ _ _

Puzzle 3

Puzzle 4

Eva is a tenacious and adventurous young girl who has a deep passion for [ACROSS 6] _ _ _ _ _ _ _ _ _. She loves nothing more than being out in the
[ACROSS 4]_ _ _ _ _ surrounded by the natural world, learning about the different types of [ACROSS 2] _ _ _ _ _ and the wildlife that calls them home.
With her trusty [ACROSS 7] _ _ _ _ _ by her side, Eva has honed her skills in bush craft and [DOWN 5] _ _ _ _ _ _ _ _ skills to perfection. She can build a [DOWN 1] _ _ _ _ _ _ _ in no time. Her knowledge of bush craft which she has learned through the [DOWN 3] _ _ _ _ _ _.

Puzzle 5

There are 6 in total

Puzzle 6

Ethan has a keen eye for detail and good memory and in his spare time likes solving [number 3] _ _ _ _ _ _ _ and making up [number 2] _ _ _ _ _ _ messages. He has not had the chance to be a [number 5]_ _ _ _ _ _ _ _ _ _ _ , at least not yet. He learnt   [number 1] _ _ _ _ _ _ _ _ _ _ from his mum who used to be in the Royal Navy and has even built his own [number 4] _ _ _ _ _ _ _ . He's very much looking forward to making new friends and learning new skills at the spy school.

Puzzle 7

```
T_ _ _ _ _ _ l
C_ _ _ _ _ _r
S_ _ _ _ _ e
P_ _ _ _ _ _ _r
C_ _ _s
G_ _ _r
```

The Ravenhall Mystery

Puzzle 8

Look at it upside down. Perhaps something is missing from the wall?

Puzzle 9

Ravenhall Manor has a long and storied history, dating back several hundred years. Originally built as a grand country estate, the manor has been home to many notable figures throughout the years, from wealthy aristocrats to famous [ACROSS 6] _ _ _ _ _ _ _ and [DOWN 4] _ _ _ _ _ _ _.

During the Second World War, Ravenhall Manor was repurposed as a [ACROSS 7]_ _ _ _ _ _ _ _ for wounded [DOWN 5]_ _ _ _ _ _ _ _ . The grand halls and spacious rooms were filled with cots and [ACROSS 2] _ _ _ _ _ _ _ equipment, and the sound of nurses' footsteps echoed through the halls day and night. Many brave men and women were treated at Ravenhall, and countless lives were saved within its walls.

After the war, Ravenhall Manor was left [DOWN 3]_ _ _ _ _ for many years, its grandeur fading and its walls falling into disrepair. But in recent years, a group of dedicated individuals have worked tirelessly to restore the manor to its former glory.

Today, Ravenhall Manor is a thriving [DOWN 1] _ _ _ _ _ _ _ _ _ _ _ _ _ for young children from all over the world. Its winding corridors and the history of the manor adds a certain sense of intrigue and wonder to every activity and lesson.

Puzzle 10

4 differences in total

91

Puzzle 11

Compare the bookshelf in both photos.

Puzzle 12

Mr. Williams had a reputation for being an expert in [A] _ _ _ _ _ _ _ _ _ _ work. He had a [F] _ _ _ _ _   _ _ _ for detail and was able to pick up on even the slightest hints of suspicious activity. He was also great at asking tough [D]   _ _ _ _ _ _ _ _ _ , able to extract valuable information from even the most stubborn of sources.

In addition, Mr. Williams was also fluent in several [B] _ _ _ _ _ _ _ _ _ , as he has travelled to many countries and met with local people. Furthermore, Mr. Williams was also an expert in the art of [5] _ _ _ _ _ _ in plain sight. He knew how to change his appearance and mannerisms to [E] _ _ _ _ _ _ _ with any crowd.

Puzzle 13

Miss Green is a master of several different forms of martial arts, including **k*****, j***,** and taekwondo. In addition to these more traditional forms of martial arts, Miss Green has also studied a variety of modern combative systems, such as Krav Maga and Brazilian Jiu-Jitsu. These disciplines have allowed her to develop a well-rounded skill set that includes grappling, striking, and ground **c******* techniques. In addition to her physical and tactical skills, Miss Green was also a **h******* and computer expert. She had spent many years working in the field of cyber espionage, using her skills to get into the enemy computer **n******** and gather valuable intelligence. She is skilled at identifying and finding weaknesses in computer systems, and can often gain **a******* to even the most heavily guarded networks.

Puzzle 14

Mr Long is the [1] _ _ _ _ _ _ _ _ _ _ _ of Ravenhall Manor. He is known for being a somewhat [2]_ _ _ _ _ _ figure, rarely being social or speaking with the students or staff unless it is absolutely necessary.

To the outside world, Mr. Long is seen as a respected [3]_ _ _ _ _ _ _ and academic, with a deep knowledge of [4]_ _ _ _ _ _ _ and a passion for education.

His knowledge of World War I and II has made him a keen [5]_ _ _ _ _ _ _ _ of wartime memorabilia such as medals and other artefacts. He is well-regarded in the academic community, and is often invited as a   [6] _ _ _ _ _ _ _ _ _ _ _ _ at conferences and other events.

Puzzle 15

Use the morse code table to replace each letter. You can do it!

Puzzle 16

The job of a spy (use the decoder table to replace the dots and dashes with a letter!)

Puzzle 17

What a great spy does

Puzzle 18

No hints for this one! Use the pigpen cipher

Puzzle 19

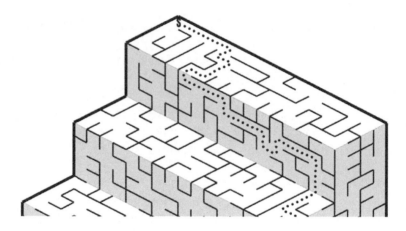

Puzzle 20

"The" is DRO

Puzzle 21

"S" = "A"

Puzzle 22

"GWC" = "YOU"

Puzzle 23

Each message on the wall is in pigpen cipher and will indicate which direction to take (using north/east/west/south) to get to a location.

Since the map is handwritten, it may be difficult to determine which coordinate each location is at.

Puzzle 24

.-/ -/ = at

Puzzle 25

C = T

N = E

Puzzle 26

Family relations

Caesar Cipher Wheel

Cut out the two discs.

Place the smaller disc on top of the bigger disc.

Make a hole in the middle of both disc.

Use a pin to secure the two discs together.

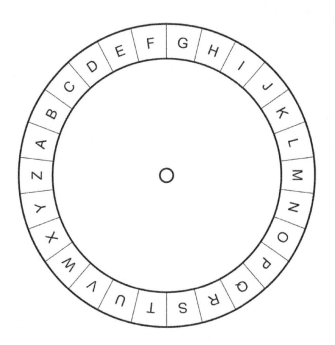

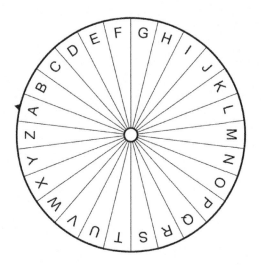

ABOUT THE AUTHOR

It was over the kitchen table that my love and interest for crosswords and puzzles would begin. My grandma and grandpa would sometimes work together, sometimes do their own crosswords. I would flit between them and "help" as best as I could.

It was the age before internet, so if we were stuck, we had to look up in a lexicon and apply some lateral thinking. Every week, we would get new, fresh crosswords and puzzles from a weekly magazine they subscribed to. My grandma would admonish my grandpa if he took the easy ones. I still remember with pride when I could finish one without their help.

They are both no longer with us, and I had forgotten about those evenings until recently. I was working on making STEM related activities for my son and his peers, when one of the parents asked if they could have the handouts for the spy and code breaking themed day. Four months later, "The Ravenhall Manor Mystery" was created.

I hope you will come along on this journey with me - this has been fun for me to do, thinking up stories and puzzles and bringing it together. I really hope I can help re-create the experience I had with my grandparents for others, and it provides something to do, whether on your own or with others, that doesn't require screen time or wifi.

L.A.Edge

Printed in Great Britain
by Amazon

31358694R00059